THE ANT BULLY

REVENGE OF THE ANTS

ADAPTED BY BENJAMIN HARPER
BASED ON THE SCREENPLAY BY JOHN A. DAVIS

SCHOLASTIC INC.

New York   Toronto   London   Auckland   Sydney
Mexico City   New Delhi   Hong Kong   Buenos Aires

First published in the UK by Scholastic Ltd, 2006
Scholastic Children's Books, Euston House, 24 Eversholt Street, London NW1 1DB, UK

ISBN 0-439-85679-5

12 11 10 9 8 7 6 5 4 3 2   6 7 8 9 10/0

Printed in the U.S.A.
First printing, July 2006

It was another busy day in the colony. All of the ants were going about their daily tasks. The foragers were foraging, the scouts were scouting, and the nurses were birthing new baby ants. Then suddenly, they felt the tremors.

The Destroyer was coming!

"It's the Destroyer!" the ants called to each other. "Run for your lives!"

The mound was in chaos. Earthquakes shook walls to the ground, and giant waves of water flooded the tunnels! Ants everywhere ran for cover.

The powerful wizard ant Zoc tried to use his magic against the Destroyer.

"Away, monster!" Zoc shouted. "I will use my powers to destroy you!"

All of a sudden, the flood stopped. Zoc's magic had worked! The Destroyer was defeated! Or was he?

BLAM! A giant shoe stomped down on the mound, sending dirt and ants flying everywhere! Then, as quickly as he had come, he was gone.

The Destroyer was a boy named Lucas. He was new to the neighborhood, and the town bully loved to pick on him. Lucas hated being teased, so he took it out on the ants. When he was feeling upset, his favorite thing to do was to spray the ant mound in his yard with the garden hose.

"Lucas!" his mother called. "Come inside and say good-bye!"

Lucas's parents were going out of town, leaving him at home with his sister and grandmother.

Lucas was blasting the ant mound again when Stan Beals, the exterminator, snuck up on him.

"I was about your age when I flooded my first colony," the exterminator told him slyly. "Your dad ordered my services, but he forgot to sign the contract before he left. He said, 'Have my son, Lucas, sign the contract for me.'"

Lucas was skeptical, but he went ahead and signed the contract. Soon his yard would be ant-free.

Meanwhile, back at the ant colony, Zoc was working on a potion to stop the Destroyer.

"Klak Teel!" he shouted.

Poof! A puff of smoke floated into the air, but nothing else happened. Zoc kept trying. He had to get it right. If not, the ants would all have to move to a new mound—and soon! The Destroyer's attacks were getting worse each day.

"Klak Teel!" Zoc shouted again.

Suddenly, the potion started glowing. It was a success!

"Praise the Mother!" Zoc shouted.

Now he could stop the Destroyer once and for all.

Lucas the Destroyer was sound asleep when the line of ants crept into his bedroom with their magic potion. Very quietly, the ants climbed up onto Lucas's bed. Zoc got very close to Lucas's ear and— *plop!* He dropped the potion inside.

BOOM! Lucas woke with a start. Something was different. His Frog Flyers game was the size of a building, and giant ants surrounded him! Lucas panicked and fell off the bed, landing on some potato chips.

"Human." One of the ants beckoned him. "Come with us."

Somehow, Lucas had shrunk down to the size of an ant!

The ants carried Lucas out of his house and to their anthill, which now looked like an enormous mountain to Lucas.

The ants brought Lucas before the Ant Council, which found him guilty of crimes against the colony.

As punishment, the Queen sentenced Lucas to learn to live as an ant.

Zoc's friend Hova told the Queen she would teach Lucas how to live like an ant.

"You must become an ant if you ever want to return home," Hova told him.

"And how am I supposed to do that?" Lucas asked.

"Well, you just have to find your place in the colony," Hova replied.

Lucas learned to be an ant the hard way. First, he had foraging class. They were searching for something the ants called sweet rocks—jelly beans! Then wasps attacked the ants. At first, Lucas ran and left Hova behind, but then he fought back. He was a hero!

Well, everyone but Zoc thought he was a hero. Zoc thought Lucas was only fighting to save himself.

After his adventure, Lucas's new friends taught him more about the ant world. They introduced him to the Ant Mother—the Queen of Queens.

Hova, Kreela, and their friend Fugax took Lucas deep within the mound to the Chamber of Ages. He saw pictures of the Ant Mother, and then pictures of one they called the Cloud Breather—a human who was breathing smoke. *The exterminator!*

Suddenly, Lucas remembered that he had signed a contract with the exterminator.

"Oh, no!" he shouted. "I've got to go home right now!"

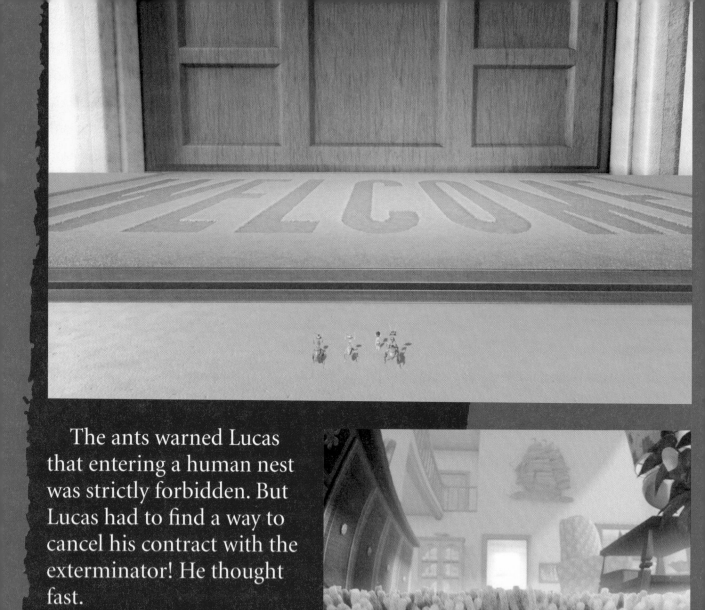

The ants warned Lucas that entering a human nest was strictly forbidden. But Lucas had to find a way to cancel his contract with the exterminator! He thought fast.

"The colony needs food, right?" he asked the ants. "Sweet rocks! My house is filled with them!"

Lucas and the ants had a hard time getting across the shag carpet to the kitchen, but when they finally did, they found tons of jelly beans!

"Oh, Lucas!" Fugax cried. "It's beautiful!"

While the ants gathered jelly beans, Lucas looked for the exterminator's phone number on the fridge. Then he ran for the phone.

"Please cancel the contract!" he shouted into the phone. "No exterminator!"

"No extra tomatoes?" a voice replied. Lucas didn't realize he had called Pizza Kingdom by mistake!

"What's an exterminator?" Hova asked.

"Don't worry," Lucas said, relieved. "Everything's okay now. Let's get out of here."

Lucas and the ants used the drain in the sink to get home.

Later that evening when he was getting a drink from a pond, a frog swallowed Lucas! Hova and Fugax chased the frog, but there was nothing they could do to save Lucas. They had to ask Zoc for help.

Zoc waved at the frog to get his attention. Then he let the frog eat him. Once he joined Lucas in the frog's belly, Zoc used a special potion to make the frog burp.

And burp he did! Out popped Lucas and Zoc!

That night, the ants camped on top of a toadstool. Zoc and Lucas stayed up talking.

"Hey, Zoc," Lucas said. "Thanks for rescuing me from the frog. Why did you do it?"

"An ant will sacrifice himself for friends," Zoc replied. He was beginning to realize that Lucas wasn't so bad after all.

"Good night, Zoc," Lucas yawned, rolling over.

"Good night, Lucas," Zoc replied.

Zoc and Lucas awoke the next morning to a great commotion. The Ant Mother was here and the ants were all celebrating her arrival.

Their joy turned to horror when they realized that the Ant Mother was actually part of the Cloud Breather's truck! The exterminator had come after all!

Lucas told the ants that the Cloud Breather's magic was strong. They had to act fast if they were going to survive.

"The potion!" Lucas cried. "*Pow!* Right in the ear!" That would shrink the exterminator down to their size.

The wasps agreed to help the ants in their battle. Ants loaded their silk squirters with the potion and then rode on the wasps' backs in formation toward their target.

"I'm going in," yelled Kreela as she zoomed toward Stan's face. "I can't get through!" she cried. Stan was wearing goggles!

"We'll have to find another way in!" said Zoc. If they didn't get that potion into the exterminator in time, they were done for!

The battle was in full force—wasps, ants, and other insects were attacking while Stan blasted them with clouds of insecticide.

Bam! Hova's wasp was hit! When they landed, Hova was pinned under the injured wasp. Lucas rushed to save her.

"Hova, are you okay?" Lucas cried.

"Save yourself!" Hova told him.

"That's not the way ants are," Lucas replied.

To Hova's amazement, Lucas lifted the wasp off of her. She was free!

Lucas returned to the fight. And he had a great idea!

Lucas dipped his wasp's stinger in Zoc's potion. Then Lucas and the wasp soared in and stung Stan!

"Yeeeeeeoooow!" the exterminator shouted. His lower body was shrinking! He rode away, vowing revenge.

Lucas and the ants had won. The colony was safe, and Lucas had finally become a true ant.